Parents' Magazine Press
A Division of Parents' Magazine Enterprises, Inc.
52 Vanderbilt Ave., New York, N. Y. 10017

HOW FAR IS FAR?

by Alvin Tresselt

illustrated by Ward Brackett

"How far is far?" asked the little boy.

"As far as the end of your nose," said his mother, and she kissed the end of his nose.

"As far as you can walk until you get tired. As far away as the other side of the world. Even as far away as the first star that shines when the sky grows dark."

"That's a lot to think about," said the little boy, and he went out to dig a hole.

"How deep is down?" asked the little boy.

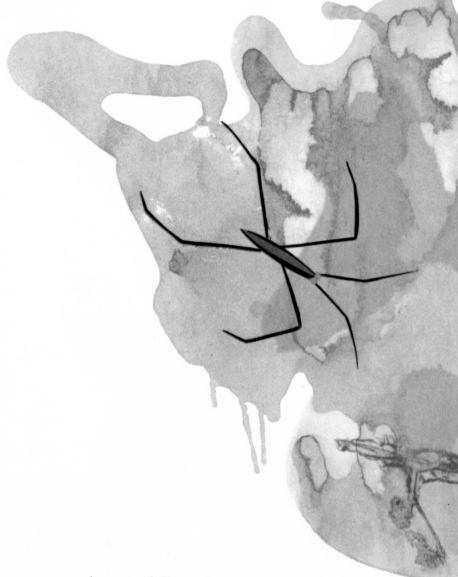

"As deep as a rain puddle after an April shower," said the water bug. He skated across the puddle to the other side.

"As deep as a rabbit's nest," said a bunny. He scampered down deep to the bottom of his warm nest.

"Deeper than my deepest roots," the old oak tree told him. "Deeper than a diamond that has never seen the sun. Deeper than the water that runs in hidden rivers under the earth."

"That's too deep for me," said the little boy, and he climbed up the apple tree, into the buzzing bees and the pink apple blossoms.

"How high is up?" asked the little boy.

"As high as the tip-top leaf at the top of the tree," said a hurrying ant. He hurried over the bark on his busy black legs, up to the tip-top leaf.

"High as a fly in the sky," twittered a swallow. He swooped over the top of the tree and caught a fly in the sky.

"High as the top of your head," said the apple tree. "High as the moon on a cold winter night. High as the sun on the longest day of the year." The apple tree shrugged its branches, and the spring breeze filled the air with a petal snowstorm.

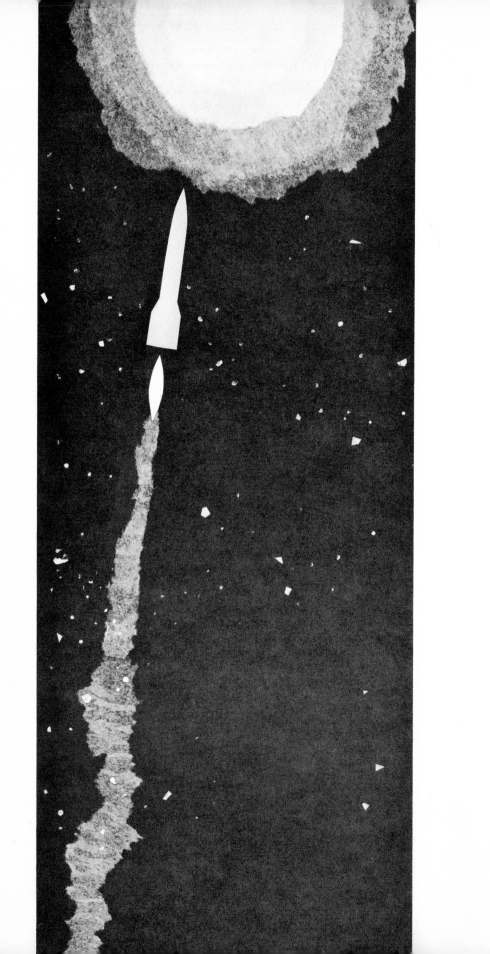

"I'll ride a rocket to the top of the sky some day," said the little boy. "Then I'll know how high is up."

He went in to talk things over with his grandmother.

"What is the sky?" asked the little boy.

"A big bowl full of clouds for a giant's breakfast," said his grandmother, with a wink.

"A place to hang stars when the sun goes down. A sea full of night for the moon to sail across while you sleep. A playground for birds and a home for the wind."

"Maybe," said the little boy, "but I think it's just a lot of blue air." And he went out to look for his cat.

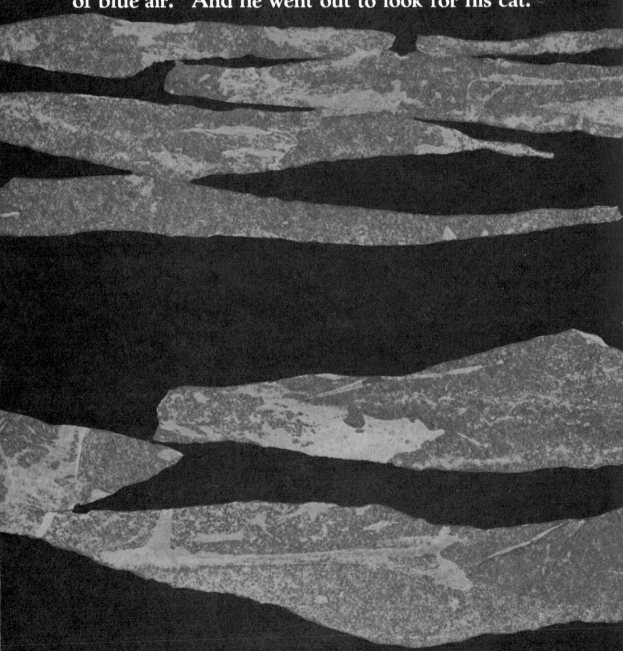

"What is the wind?" he asked the cat, as the wind ruffled the fur on her back. The cat looked very wise, as only cats can, and licked her fur into place again.

"The wind teaches the leaves to speak," said the cat, looking down her nose. "It waves the branches to and fro, and the leaves talk about the weather in rustly voices . . .

The wind brings the cold from the northland, and it tells the birds it's time to fly away. Then it carries back the smell of spring in its arms. It touches your cheek with a gentle kiss . . .

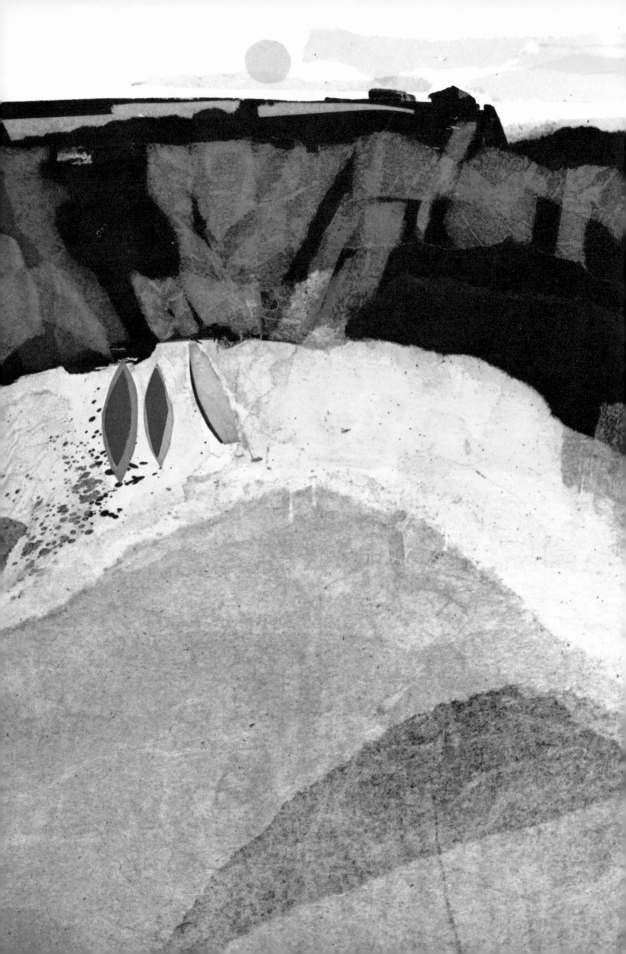

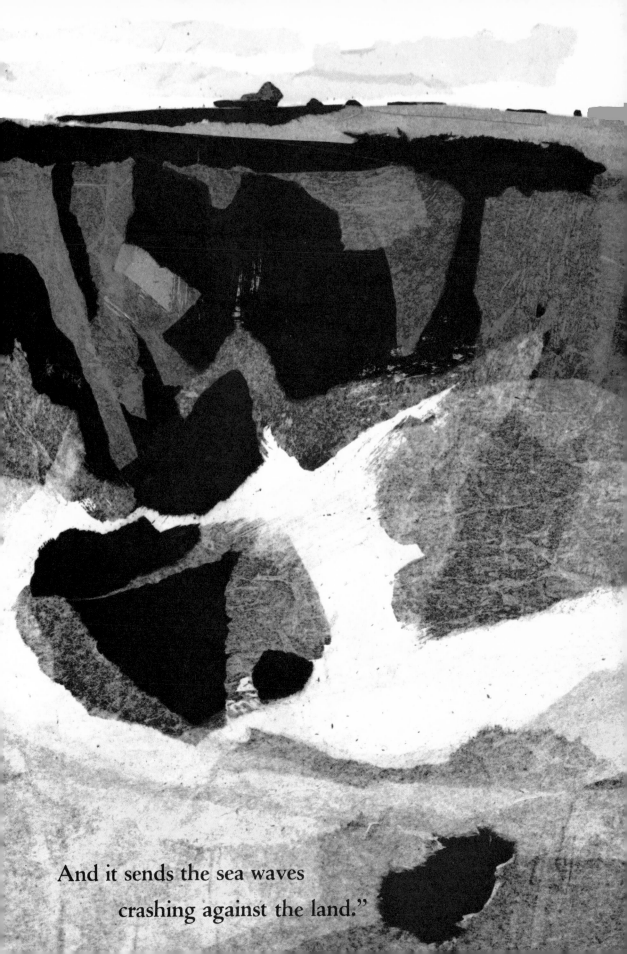

And it sends the sea waves
crashing against the land."

The cat waved her tail in the air as she picked her way across the tickly grass. "It also ruffles my fur when I face the wrong way," she said crossly, and she went about her secret cat business.

"Cats think they know everything," said the little boy, and he ran to say hello to his father who had just come home.

"How big is big?" asked the little boy, as his father swung him up in the air in his big strong arms.

"As big as your eyes at your birthday party," said his father.

"As big as a baby bird that is big enough to fly . . .

As big as a house full of people . . .

As big as the billion, billion drops of water that fill the ocean . . .

As big as a little boy who will grow into a man and have a little boy of his own." Then his father carried him into the house on his big broad shoulders.

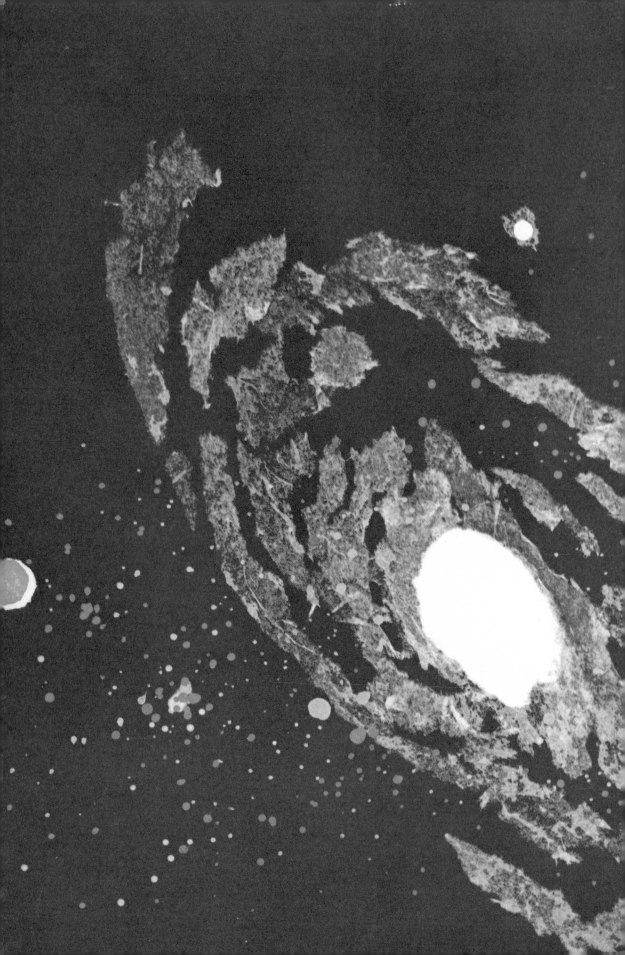